AXEL STORM

DIAMOND MOON

For Rueben and Thomas

ORCHARD BOOKS
338 Euston Road, London NW1 3BH
Orchard Books Australia
Level 17/207 Kent Street, Sydney, NSW 2000

First published in 2010
First paperback publication in 2011

ISBN 978 1 40830 259 0 (hardback)
ISBN 978 1 40830 267 5 (paperback)

Text and illustrations © Shoo Rayner 2010

A CIP catalogue record for this book is available
from the British Library.

1 3 5 7 9 10 8 6 4 2 (hardback)
1 3 5 7 9 10 8 6 4 2 (paperback)

Printed in Great Britain

Orchard Books is a division of Hachette Children's Books,
an Hachette UK company.

AXEL STORM

DIAMOND MOON

SHOO RAYNER

ORCHARD BOOKS

CHAPTER ONE

"There's nothing to watch on TV," Axel Storm complained as he flicked through the seven hundred channels on the luxury hotel entertainment system. "I'm going to get so bored while we're staying here."

"You'll have lots to do tomorrow at Celebrity Kids' Club," Mum chirped. "You can make some nice new friends."

"Yow!" Axel leapt off the sofa as though a million volts of electricity had been plugged into his body. "I'm not going to Celebrity Kids' Club!" Axel meant it. He stood firm, hands on hips, his right eyebrow raised in defiance.

"I'm sorry, but we've got a million things to do before the Grand Opening of the museum," Dad explained. "Mum's got to get her hair done and try on her dress. There are photo shoots and interviews to do. We won't have a spare minute to look after you."

"Can't I help?" Axel asked hopefully.

"What? And have people taking pictures of you for the newspapers?" Mum trilled. "We want to keep you out of the spotlight so you can grow up like a normal child."

Axel's Mum and Dad were rock stars.

Their band, Stormy Skies, had recorded twenty-two platinum-selling hits in eighty-three different countries around the world. They spent half their lives travelling, performing concerts and meeting their millions of fans.

"There aren't any normal children at Celebrity Kids' Club," Axel moaned. "Last time I went there, Nina Gonzales, the Formula One racing driver's daughter, nearly ran me over in her pedal car. And Master Universe, the junior weight-lifting champion, wouldn't put me down for two weeks!"

"Axel, you know how important this museum is to your mum. The Diamond Moon is the star exhibit! There will be masses of security guards at the opening," Dad explained. "I'm afraid you might get in the way."

The Storms were so rich that one Valentine's Day, Dad had given Mum the most expensive diamond in the world.

Mum had named it the Diamond
Moon, because it was round and glowed
like the moon. It had also been a full
moon when Dad had given it to her on
the beach on their private island in the
Bahamas. Dad had always been a bit of
an old romantic!

The trouble with owning something so expensive is that you have to find somewhere safe to keep it. If you put it in a drawer under the stairs, or in a box under your bed, all the diamond thieves in the world will try to break in and steal it.

So Mum's diamond had been sitting in a bank vault ever since.

Along with…Dad's antique guitars…

...his Ancient Egypt collection...

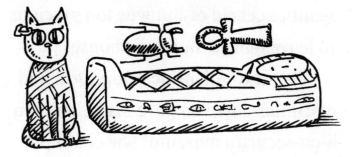

...three Picasso paintings...

...tons of jewellery that Mum
never wore...

...and all the other stuff that they didn't want to get rid of but was too precious to leave lying around the house.

The next Valentine's Day, Dad had a brilliant idea: he gave Mum her own high-security museum! She could put everything inside, keep it safe and look at it whenever she wanted to. All their fans could come and see everything, too!

The Storms were staying at a luxury hotel for the *Sky Storm Museum* Grand Opening. Mum was going to cut the ribbon as the museum was named after her.

Just then, Dad's phone beeped.

"You've got a text message from Uncle Raffles," Axel said, picking the phone up from the table and passing it to him.

"CU IN 1." Dad read the message out slowly. "What on earth does that mean?" he grumbled. "I can never understand text messages."

"It means, *See you in one minute*," Axel laughed.

As he spoke, the balcony doors slid open silently. The rich, heavy curtains billowed in the warm spring breeze.

A tall, dark, mysterious man stood silhouetted against the evening sky.

How on earth did he get there? wondered Axel. The hotel suite was on the thirty-second floor!

CHAPTER TWO

"What the…!" Axel stammered. "Where did you come from?"

The man sauntered into the room and ruffled Axel's hair.

"Hello, Axel!" he chirped. "My, haven't you grown?"

Axel rolled his eyes skywards. Why did grown-ups always say that?

Uncle Raffles said hello to Mum and Dad, then he stood back and looked at his nephew again. "Actually," he said, "you haven't grown *that* much – have you, Axel?"

He walked round Axel three times, as if he was examining a racehorse.

"Hmmm. Can I borrow Axel for a couple of days?" he asked. "I've almost finished testing the museum security, but I think Axel could really help me. I need someone his size to put the system through its final checks."

No one knew what Uncle Raffles actually did. All they really knew was that he had been helping Mum and Dad make sure that the new museum was absolutely secure.

The designers had said that no one could break in, and if they did, they would never be able to escape. Uncle Raffles had been checking all the things the designers hadn't thought of.

"Can I, Mum? Can I, Dad? Please, please, ple-e-e-ease?" Axel put his hands together, fluttered his eyelashes and begged shamelessly. "It sounds so much more *educational* than Celebrity Kids' Club," he suggested.

Uncle Raffles winked at Axel. "Oh, yes!" he agreed. "It'll be very *educational*!"

"We-e-ll...I suppose so," Mum
sighed. "As long as you keep Axel away
from photographers. Archie Flash from
Celebrity Gossip Magazine is in town.
We certainly don't want Axel's picture
in the papers."

"Keeping things secret is my job,"
Uncle Raffles said mysteriously.

"OK," Dad nodded, "but we don't
want Axel getting up to any of his wild
adventures."

"It's a deal," said Uncle Raffles.

"Yahoo!" Axel whooped.

Uncle Raffles walked out onto the balcony. "Meet me here at eight-thirty tomorrow morning," he said.

Then…he was gone!

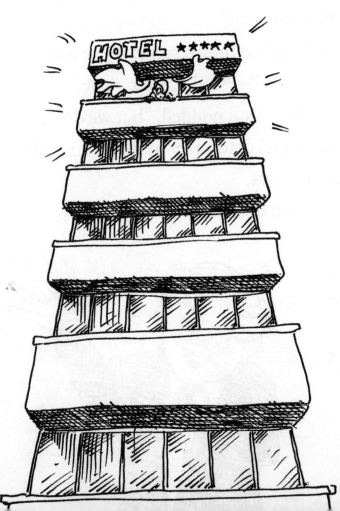

CHAPTER THREE

The next day, Axel was ready and waiting. At exactly eight-thirty, a coil of rope dropped out of the sky. Seconds later, Uncle Raffles slid down the rope, landing on the balcony as lightly as a cat.

He handed Axel a harness. "Ready?"

"I'm ready for anything," Axel grinned.

Uncle Raffles checked that their harnesses were nice and tight, then he helped Axel climb onto the edge of the balcony.

Mum appeared just in time to see them balanced on the balcony – thirty-two floors up! Axel glimpsed her horrified stare as Uncle Raffles counted to three and they hurled themselves into the air.

"AXEL!" Mum screamed. "Come back here right no-o-o-w…" Her voice faded as Axel hurtled down the side of the building.

The deafening sound of air rushing past his ears stopped abruptly. Axel's body jerked upwards as the paraglider canopy snapped open. "This is amazing, Uncle Raffles!" he yelled.

"Remember to steer with the ropes and follow me," Uncle Raffles called back.

They flew across the city like eagles, twisting and turning above the streets, kept aloft by rising currents of warm air from cars and air-conditioning systems.

They spiralled down into a park, landing gracefully in the middle of a tennis court. The tennis players stood open-mouthed as Uncle Raffles calmly packed their canopies into backpacks.

"Sorry!" Uncle Raffles called cheerfully.

At the park's adventure playground, Uncle Raffles put Axel through his paces. He made Axel squeeze through tunnels…

…zip down the death slide…

...scramble up the climbing wall...and abseil down again.

"You've passed the test," Uncle Raffles said. "You've got the job if you want it."

Axel was dangling from a rope, a couple of metres in the air. "What job?" He looked surprised.

"I want you to break into the Sky Storm museum and steal the Diamond Moon!"

Axel's jaw dropped open. "Me? Steal?"

"Well, it's not really stealing, is it?"
Uncle Raffles smiled. "Not from your
own family – and you'll give it back,
won't you? You'll just be checking the
last weak point in the security system.
We'll break in after it gets dark tonight."
Uncle Raffles winked at Axel. "So, do
you want the job, or not?"

"Oh, yes! This beats Celebrity Kids'
Club any day!"

Suddenly, Uncle Raffles tensed. He screwed up his eyes and focused all his attention on the bushes nearby.

"Wait here!" he hissed. Axel watched in amazement as his uncle burst into action. Racing across the grass, he hurled himself into the bushes. After a good deal of shouting and grumbling, and shaking of leaves and branches, he reappeared holding a man by the scruff of the neck.

"It's Archie Flash," Axel sighed. "He follows me everywhere. He'll be cooking up a story about me for *Celebrity Gossip Magazine*."

Archie grinned. He could always smell a good story about Axel. "I was watching the hotel when I saw you two leap off the balcony. I wasn't going to miss that story, was I? I jumped into a taxi and told the driver to follow the paragliders!"

Uncle Raffles stood toe to toe with Archie and stared deep into his eyes. "Well, you'd better find another taxi and get out of here right now," he growled menacingly. "Otherwise I'll..."

Archie Flash didn't wait to find out what Uncle Raffles would do to him. With a big smile on his face, he ran off towards the park gates. "See you later!" he called.

"I'd better not!" Uncle Raffles snarled.

CHAPTER FOUR

Uncle Raffles and Axel spent the rest of the day poring over plans of the museum and rehearsing their strategy.

"We can get in through the air-conditioning system," Uncle Raffles explained. "There's a big fan on the roof that blows air into the building. You are just small enough to squeeze between the blades of the fan. That's the last weak point in the whole building."

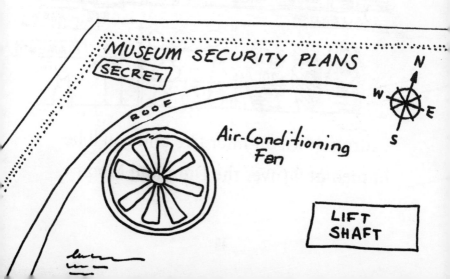

"Blades!" Axel squeaked. "Won't
I get cut in half?"

"The air conditioning is turned off at
night, so you'll be able to slip through.
Now, remember this: drop down twenty
metres...

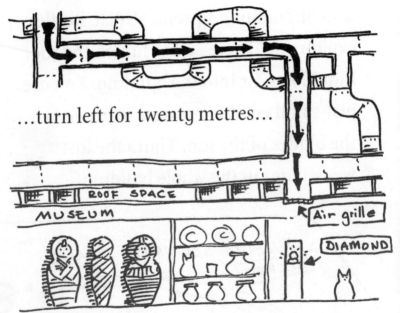

...turn left for twenty metres...

ROOF SPACE

MUSEUM

Air grille

DIAMOND

...drop down another five and you'll be
immediately over the Diamond Moon...

"Then all you have to do is open
the air grille, abseil down, remove the
diamond and get back to the roof before
the fan starts up again...simple!"

Almost too simple, Axel thought.
"Aren't there laser beams and trip wires
and things?" he asked.

"No," Uncle Raffles grinned. "The
designers are so sure that no one can get
in or out of the museum when it's closed,
they haven't installed anything like that
at all. We're going to give them a big
surprise before anyone else does."

Axel learnt how to unscrew the grille and set up the ropes to abseil down. He practised all afternoon until he felt confident that he knew exactly what to do.

"I'm going to write the directions on the back of my hand, so I don't lose them," he said.

"Good boy!" his uncle smiled. "Now you're thinking like a professional."

CHAPTER FIVE

The sky turned dark and the city streets grew quiet. Two figures slipped down the side of the museum and disappeared into the shadows.

Uncle Raffles tossed a rope into the sky. The grappling hook clanged and snagged on the metal fire-escape ladder. He gently pulled it down to the ground.

The ladder creaked and groaned as they crept up to the roof. They crouched in the shadows and waited beside the huge air-conditioning fan.

The giant fan blades roared. They raced round and round, making Axel shiver at the thought of climbing in between them.

At eight o'clock sharp, something clicked and the fan motor switched off. The heavy blades throbbed and swished as they cut through the air. They swept round under their own weight, again and again, getting slower and slower until finally they shuddered to a halt.

Silence descended on the roof. Far below, car horns hooted and trains rattled.

"It's now or never," Uncle Raffles whispered. "Are you ready?"

Axel took a deep breath. He wondered if this was one adventure too many. Mum and Dad would go mad if they knew what he was doing!

"I'm ready!" he answered quietly.

An electric screwdriver soon loosened the bolts that held the safety grille on the fan. The blades looked sharp and unforgiving. Axel slipped a metal clip onto his harness and tightened up the safety lock.

Uncle Raffles patted him on the back. "Good luck, son. See you back here soon. If anything goes wrong I'll pull you out before you can say *Diamond Moon*."

CHAPTER SIX

Slipping between the fan blades was a tight squeeze. It was even tighter in the air duct, as Axel let himself down. He was glad he'd worn his woolly hat because he kept banging his head on the walls of the duct.

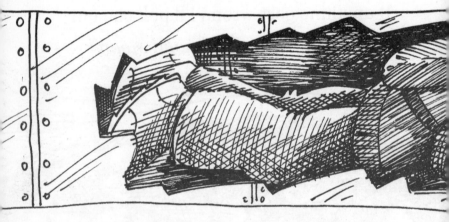

The rope was marked with red electrical tape, so he knew when he had dropped down the first twenty metres.

His torchlight revealed an opening to one side.

"This must be the left turn," he muttered, scrambling into the new duct. Twenty metres on, he dropped down another five metres. He found himself directly above the grille, just as Uncle Raffles had said he would.

A strange light glowed from the grille.
Axel peered through the holes. The
Diamond Moon glittered right below him.
Axel caught his breath. This felt like
a dream!

It was very narrow in the air duct,
but Axel found his tools and carefully
unscrewed the bolts on the grille. He
slowly removed it, making an Axel-sized
opening right above the fabulous jewel.

Uncle Raffles had kitted out Axel with powerful suction hooks, which he now stuck to the ceiling of the air duct. He looped rope around the hooks and lowered himself through the hole.

Axel hung in the air, turning slowly. He could hear his own heartbeat.

Axel felt very exposed, as if the whole world was watching him! But they weren't. He was all on his own.

The room was dimly lit from the weak glow of the emergency exit lights. Dad's Ancient Egypt collection lined the walls – including several mummys' tombs. It was quite creepy.

The rope creaked as Axel descended centimetre by centimetre.

The diamond sat on a blue cushion inside a plexiglass box on top of a metal column, which was bolted to the floor.

There was a hole in the cushion
through which a light shone, making the
jewel sparkle and glow. Its beauty was
hypnotising.

Axel loosened the screws that held
the plexiglass box in place. Carefully,
he lifted the cover off the base. Then he
reached out and took the diamond from
its soft cushion.

A loud, jarring, creaking groan made Axel spin round. The lid of a mummy's tomb was opening slowly, its ancient hinges complaining loudly.

"Say cheese!" A brilliant, dazzling light blazed in front of Axel. He was blinded for a moment, but he knew that voice – Archie Flash!

"I heard you and your uncle planning everything," Archie laughed. "So I hid in the mummy's tomb and waited until closing time. It's a great story. Thanks, Axel!"

Axel's only thought was to get out as quickly as possible before he was caught red-handed. He didn't want to go to jail for being a jewel thief! He hauled himself up the ropes and scrambled back into the air duct. He wriggled and climbed his way to the main shaft.

"Uncle Raffles! Help!" Axel yelled.

Axel felt himself being hauled up the shaft. Above him, he saw the silhouette of the vicious fan blades.

Axel was almost there when the alarms began ringing. That same moment, something clicked and the fan began to hum noisily.

"Quick!" Axel shouted.

Uncle Raffles grabbed him and
pulled him out just as the heavy, sharp
blades began to turn.

"Did you get the diamond?" Uncle
Raffles asked in an urgent whisper.

Axel reached into his inside pocket
and pulled out the Diamond Moon.
He held it up to show his uncle. The
city lights twinkled all around them,
repeated a thousand times in the
diamond's many brilliant faces.

Uncle Raffles laughed and hugged
Axel tightly. "Nice work!"

CHAPTER SEVEN

A day later, after the Grand Opening of the museum, Mum and Dad spread all the newspapers across the floor of their hotel suite.

"I don't believe it," Dad complained. "The whole Grand Opening doesn't get more than a quarter of a page in any of the papers."

Mum was upset, too. "They don't even have a full-length picture of me in my dress!" she moaned.

"…and Axel gets a ten-page photo special about how he managed to steal the Diamond Moon!" Dad glowered at his son. Once again, Axel's adventures had made the headlines.

Axel stared innocently out of the window. "We were only checking that the museum was safe," he said. "You wouldn't have liked it if real jewel thieves had broken in, would you?"

"Oh, Axel," Mum sighed. "What are we going to do with you? All we want is for you to be like any other normal boy."

"I am normal!" Axel protested. "I was only helping out a favourite uncle. How normal is that?"

CELEBRITY
GOSSIP
MAGAZINE

AXEL STORMS MUSEUM
JUNIOR INTERNATIONAL CRIMINAL MASTERMIND!

AXEL STORM was caught in the act of stealing his mother's priceless gem, the Diamond Moon, the night before the official Grand Opening of the Sky Storm Museum. Why isn't Axel behind the bars of a high-security jail? Police sources tell us he was only testing the museum security system. Museum Security Chief, Raffles Storm, who is Axel's uncle, has now declared the museum

"SAFE AS HOUSES"

after installing extra security measures. Raffles said of his nephew: "That boy is a diamond!"

By ace reporter, Archie Flash.

SHOO RAYNER

ALL PRICED AT £8.99

Orchard Books are available from all good bookshops,
or can be ordered from our website: www.orchardbooks.co.uk,
or telephone 01235 827702, or fax 01235 827703.